TEDDY
Takes a Train

Teddy was sitting aloft, high in his favourite tree,
Enjoying a pot of honey, for his afternoon tea.
Suddenly from far below, he heard a cheerful cry,
It was Jimbo, Bessy and Belle who were walking by.

Teddy quickly swung down
        to greet his good friends the bears.
Then all sat down together,
        using logs for chairs.
Teddy Bear said: "I've been thinking.
        About all sorts of things today.
And I've had a good idea,
        for a trip on a train away-day."

"What a very good idea." They all at once agreed,
"Yes, a trip on a train, would be very nice indeed."
Bessy and Belle exclaimed, "But wherever shall we go?"
"To Teddy Town," said Teddy, "it's really nice you know."

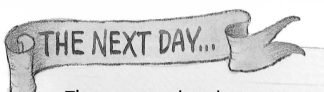

They arrived at the station just before eight,
  The bears all hoping their train would not be late.
They waited and listened to hear the train whistle: "Hello."
  Then it puffed into the station—what a magnificent show!

The engine was painted, in a bright red and green,
There was black smoke puffing and a hissing of steam.
The engine huffed, puffed and snorted with impatient glee,
As it pulled six green carriages up to platform three.

The bears with tickets ready, stepped up on board,
  The carriage doors banged shut, then the engine roared.
CLICKETY-CLICK, CLICKETY-CLACK THE TRAIN WENT
  CHUGGING DOWN THE TRACK.
Woo-Woo whistled the train as it sped on its way,
  Teddy clapped paws and whooped: "Oh what a lovely day."

The train rattled along speeding over the rails,
      Past villages and farms, over hills and
                     through dales.
At last in high spirits, they arrived at
      Teddy Town Station,
And alighted on the platform,
      with great anticipation.

They went to the museum, of Ancient Bear Art,
    where they saw a nice picture, of an ox and a cart.
It was by Constable Bear, and was called "The Haywain".
    Bessy said,"It's beautiful, we must come here again."

Then they went to the zoo,
    to see the animals there,
There were lots of friendly creatures and some
    were quite rare.
They bought some postcards, of their friends
    in the zoo.
And Teddy then sent one, to Winnie the Pooh!

At lunch time Jimbo said, "I'm ready to eat,"
      So they bought some ice-creams, as a special treat.
They each had a choc-bar, with nuts on the top,
      Then each had a glass, of orange fizzy-pop!

The bears then decided
        they would go to the fair,
Where they each bought a balloon
        from nice Grizzly Bear.
Jimbo chose a red one,
        Teddy chose a blue,
Bessy chose a pink one
        and so did Belle too.

They went on the dodgems and then on a big slide,
Then hurtled all around on a moon rocket ride.

They went on the big wheel high above the ground,
Then on the big dipper which went all around.

Then on to the hoop-la,
for prizes to win,
Jimbo threw first,
and won a lovely cake tin.

Bessy won a ball,
Teddy won a bat,
And Belle won a big
red feathery hat!

The Bears went on the ghost train,
    Then into the haunted house,
Belle screamed at the top of her voice,
    when she saw a little field mouse.
He said his name was Fred and
    he had been living there a year.
He was dining off some cheese
    and the very best ginger-beer.

GHOST TRAIN

But now the bears were hungry
and the time was getting late,
"Let's have a nice fish and chip supper.
Not in the paper, but on a plate."
So they went to the Sea-Shell restaurant,
the nicest one in town.
Where they had a feast of fish and chips,
with tea to wash it down.

And thus fortified the bears set forth,
        Their homeward train to catch.
Jimbo gave his balloon to Belle,
        Her feathery hat to match.

As they neared the station happily, they saw
        their friends from school.
There were David, Katy and Lucy and Joshua
        and Saul!
They boarded the train at six-thirty, sitting
        together inside.
The sun was sinking slowly, as in the train
        they began to ride.

They arrived back home so happy
and without any worries or cares.
Their Mummies and Daddies were waiting
for the tired little Teddy Bears.